The Boxcar Children M[ysteries]

THE BASKETBALL MYSTERY

created by
GERTRUDE CHANDLER WARNER

Illustrated by Charles Tang

SCHOLASTIC INC.
New York Toronto London Auckland Sydney
Mexico City New Delhi Hong Kong

ISBN 0-590-68716-6

Copyright © 1998 by Albert Whitman & Company. All rights reserved. Published by Scholastic Inc., 555 Broadway, New York, NY 10012 by arrangement with Albert Whitman & Company. BOXCAR CHILDREN is a registered trademark of Albert Whitman & Company.

12 11 10 9 8 7 6 5 4 3   9/9 0 1 2 3/0

Printed in the U.S.A.   40
First Scholastic printing, January 1999

Contents

CHAPTER 1

Turnovers and Twins

"Over here! Pass it to me!" Benny Alden yelled, waving his arms. He and his sister Violet just needed one more basket to break the tie.

Violet looked over at Benny. She looked down at Soo Lee. Her five-year-old cousin was right beside her. Violet was quick. With both hands, she passed the ball to Benny.

Soo Lee scooted after it. Too late! Benny caught the ball. He took aim and arched it into the basket!

"Eight to ten. You won!" Benny's older

brother, Henry, yelled from across the drive-way. "Soo Lee and I will get you next time."

The Aldens' backyard basketball game was over. The children plopped down on the cool grass next to twelve-year-old Jessie Alden, who had sat out this game. Their dog, Watch, waited for someone to roll him the ball. He liked basketball, too!

"Henry's the basketball champ in high school," Benny said, "but we're the champs in Grandfather's driveway. I like our new basketball stand. It's not too tall. The net over the garage is for big kids. But this one is just right for me and Soo Lee."

"You two are going to catch up to the rest of us in no time," Jessie said. "Then watch out, everybody!" She pushed the basketball across the grass with her foot. Watch chased after it. He pushed the ball back to Jessie with his nose. She rolled it to him again.

"Soo Lee was just like a little shadow guarding me," Violet told everyone.

"Speaking of shadows, look at that." Henry pointed to a long shadow moving up the sunny driveway.

Watch saw the shadow, too. He let the basketball roll down the driveway. He ran after the shadow instead.

The Aldens heard the fast, pleasant thump of a basketball hitting the driveway. Then, swoosh! The ball sailed right into the big net over the garage.

"Who threw that?" Jessie asked.

The children looked down the driveway. The sun was in their eyes. All they saw were two skinny shadows crisscrossing each other.

The Aldens heard a young woman's voice. "That's okay, Watch. We're friends."

Watch yipped and yapped and ran in circles. He liked these people with the long shadows.

The Aldens scrambled up from the grass. The two strangers dribbled and ran and jumped. They shot baskets from up close, from down the driveway, from behind their backs. They didn't miss a single shot.

The Aldens looked at one another. Who were these basketball wizards?

The children heard the screen door bang.

Grandfather Alden stood on the back porch. He smiled at the young woman and the young man. Both of them were tall, brown-haired, and fast on their feet.

"Do you know them, Grandfather?" Benny asked. "They just showed up and started shooting baskets in our yard."

Mr. Alden broke into a big smile. "You know the surprise guests that Mrs. McGregor's been baking for? Well, here they are!"

The young man and woman stopped playing. They shook hands with Mr. Alden.

"Sorry, Mr. Alden. We got carried away when we saw the basketball roll down your driveway," the young woman said. "Buzz and I just had to try it out after being cooped up in our car."

"Come meet our mystery guests," Mr. Alden said to the children. "Buzz, Tipper, these are my grandchildren. Let's start with Henry, who's fourteen. This one is Jessie, who's twelve. That's Violet, our ten-year-old. All three of them play basketball on our neighborhood teams."

"What about us?" Soo Lee asked.

Mr. Alden patted the little Korean girl's head. "Why, of course, I would never leave you out, Soo Lee. This is Cousin Joe and Cousin Alice's daughter. And last but not least, here's Benny. He's six now. He and Soo Lee are catching up to my older grand-children in basketball. I just bought them that junior-size stand to practice with. Children, meet Buzz and Tipper Nettleton."

Henry's eyes opened wide. "Are you the famous Nettleton twins?"

The young woman laughed. "Sometimes we're the not-so-famous Nettleton twins, too!"

"Wow!" Henry shook the twins' hands. "I've seen your names all over our Hall of Fame board at school. My high school coach sometimes plays old tapes of your championship basketball games."

"My coach does, too." Jessie held her hand out to Tipper Nettleton. "She said ever since you played for Greenfield High, lots more girls sign up for basketball. Congratulations on winning the Most Valuable Player trophy. Nobody from Greenfield ever won it before."

Tipper smiled. "Thanks. Buzz and I both love basketball. It's a great game —"

"Enough basketball talk," the young man said, interrupting his sister. "I'd better get our luggage, Tip."

Now the Aldens noticed another shadow. This one seemed to pass over Tipper Nettleton's smiling face.

"Sorry, did I say something wrong?" Jessie asked after Buzz and Grandfather Alden left. "It's true, though. You really are the most famous basketball player from Greenfield."

Tipper put her finger to her lips. "Sometimes it's better not to talk too much about that. Up until I won the MVP trophy last month, Buzz and I have always been proud of each other. But I think he's getting a little tired of hearing about my award."

The Aldens were surprised to hear this. They were always happy when someone in their family won something. But they were polite children and didn't say another word.

Everyone headed out front to help Buzz and Mr. Alden with the luggage.

Benny and Soo Lee picked up Buzz's big sports bag.

"That's the name of your college, right?" Benny asked when he saw the bright orange letters on the bag. "I can read."

"And I can carry heavy things," Soo Lee said. She and Benny each lifted one end of the sports bag. "Benny and I help the teams."

Buzz cheered up a little when he heard this. "Well, Tipper and I could use a couple of good helpers. We came to coach some of the neighborhood teams. That's one of the reasons your grandfather invited us to visit."

Henry lifted a suitcase from the trunk. "I heard you two were coming to Greenfield, but I didn't know you'd be staying with us! Maybe you can give us some good basketball tips."

Buzz finally started smiling again. "That's why we're here."

Grandfather closed the trunk. "Buzz and

Tipper are too modest. They've also offered to play in a fund-raising game for the new sports center on the center's Opening Day. And there's one last surprise. Should I tell them, Tipper?"

Benny and Soo Lee tugged Mr. Alden's sleeve. "Another surprise?"

Mr. Alden had a hard time keeping secrets from his grandchildren. "Tipper is donating her Most Valuable Player trophy to the new sports center. The mayor will be coming and perhaps television people as well. Now, what do you children think of that?"

"Neat!" Jessie said. "We'll have a big basketball day in Greenfield."

Soo Lee put down her end of the sports bag. She looked up at Tipper. "This is heavy. Is your trophy in here?"

Before Tipper could answer, Buzz picked up the bag. "This is *my* bag. If you want to help Tipper, you can carry her bag instead."

Benny and Soo Lee didn't know what to say. They weren't used to cross words. They watched Buzz head up the porch stairs with his sports bag and suitcase.

Tipper spoke to the children softly. "You know what? I'll show you my trophy some other time. Buzz is . . . uh . . . tired after our long drive."

The children led Tipper into the big white house where they now lived with their grandfather. Awhile back, after their parents had died, the children had lived in a boxcar in the woods. After Grandfather found them there, he brought them home to his house, with its comfy beds and delicious meals. As a surprise, he had brought the boxcar home. Now it was a playhouse in the backyard.

"Welcome," a white-haired woman called out cheerily when she saw Tipper. "I'm Mrs. McGregor, the Aldens' housekeeper. When I first met you and Buzz, you were just two little babies in a carriage. Mr. Alden told me that your father and grandfather were famous Greenfield players, too. I guess it runs in the family."

"So does being tall." Tipper ducked her head under the kitchen doorway so she wouldn't bang her forehead.

"Well, you must be hungry after your long drive to Greenfield. Come try some of my apple turnovers. I've been hiding them from Benny," Mrs. McGregor said with a wink. "I just sent your brother upstairs. He said he needed a rest. I told him to take the front guest room. I made up the guest bed for you in Jessie's bedroom."

Tipper heard a door bang upstairs. "Thank you so much, Mrs. McGregor. That will be fine. Buzz is tired from our trip."

"Are you tired?" Mr. Alden asked. "We can hold off on Mrs. McGregor's treats until you rest up."

Tipper pulled out a chair. She stretched her long legs under the kitchen table. "I'm more hungry than tired. Apple turnovers are one of my favorite things."

"I know what turnovers are," Benny announced. "They're something to eat. And know what else? There are turnovers in basketball, too, but not the kind you eat!"

Tipper's face brightened when she heard this. "Good for you, Benny! A basketball turnover happens after a player makes a mistake and the other team gets the ball."

"An apple turnover happens after Mrs. McGregor bakes," Benny said. "Then the turnovers go to us!"

Everyone laughed at Benny's joke.

Mr. Alden raised his coffee cup. "Here's to Tipper Nettleton, the Most Valuable Player in the country."

The children clinked their milk glasses against Tipper's glass and Mr. Alden's cup.

Everyone was quiet as they ate. They heard Buzz's footsteps in the guest room overhead.

Benny brushed some crumbs from his lips. "Mmm. Buzz is sure missing something good."

Tipper put down her glass. "Buzz has been missing a lot of good things lately. Every time someone mentions my trophy, he makes an excuse to get away."

This surprised Henry. "I thought twins never got jealous of each other."

Tipper smiled a little. "Buzz and I never had a smidgen of jealousy between us until now. After all, Buzz plays men's basketball, and I play on a women's team. Buzz has always been my biggest fan, and I'm his."

"So why isn't Buzz happy for you now?" Jessie wanted to know.

Tipper went on, "My trophy seems to be the problem. Winning it made me happy, but it was hard for Buzz."

Mr. Alden stirred his coffee and turned to Tipper. "Ah, yes. Your grandfather mentioned that you hope to study medicine after college. I understand Buzz plans to continue playing basketball. I suppose the Most Valuable Player trophy would have helped him more than it will help you."

Tipper stared down at her plate. "Exactly. That's why I'm donating it to the sports center. Buzz won't have to see it around all the time."

"There, there," Mrs. McGregor said kindly. "Finish your turnover. You'll feel better. You don't know these children. Why, they'll make Buzz forget all about that trophy."

Suddenly Tipper pushed back her chair. "The trophy! I didn't see anyone bring it in.

Besides being valuable to me, it's worth a lot of money. It's made out of silver."

The Aldens followed Tipper out to the car. Tipper unlocked the trunk. "It's not here! I thought Buzz put it behind the suitcases. Wait, I'd better ask him about it."

Tipper was gone in a flash. A couple of minutes later, she was back. "He said it's in the backseat."

Benny and Soo Lee went around to the side of the car.

"There's something shiny on the floor!" Benny yelled. "See?"

Tipper looked through the car window. "Whew! That's it. I'll unlock the door."

But Tipper didn't have to unlock anything. When she pulled the handle, the door opened right away. "I can't believe Buzz didn't lock the car. Thank goodness no one saw the trophy. If it were missing, it would spoil all the plans for the dedication of the sports center. I'm going to put this in a safe place. I don't want anything to happen to it before I give it to the sports center on Opening Day."

CHAPTER 2

Something Borrowed

Tha-thump! Tha-thump! Tha-thump!

"What's going on?" Jessie asked when she heard Watch at her bedroom window early the next morning.

Watch had stuck his head under the window shade to see what was making the noise outside. All Jessie could see were his hind legs and his tail wagging back and forth.

When the thumping stopped, Jessie heard voices.

"Okay, Henry, just use your fingertips to control the ball while you run."

"Basketball?" Jessie said, stretching out. "So early in the morning?"

She looked across the room. Tipper had already made up the guest bed and gone downstairs, Jessie guessed.

Watch pulled at Jessie's covers.

"I know. I know," Jessie said. "You want to be out playing basketball, too."

In no time, Jessie was dressed in shorts and sneakers. Watch raced ahead to the kitchen. Mrs. McGregor was sliding a muffin tin from the oven. The kitchen table was set for company.

"Oh, I forgot," Jessie said. "Those basketball people are coming over to meet with Tipper and Buzz."

Jessie looked out the kitchen window. Tipper was giving Benny, Soo Lee, and Violet some basketball lessons. Buzz was still helping Henry.

Mr. Alden came into the kitchen for his morning cup of coffee. "No sleeping in today, right, Jessie? Looks as if the Nettletons have started an Alden Basketball Clinic in our own backyard."

Mrs. McGregor set the warm muffins on a plate. "Benny and Soo Lee asked Buzz for lessons first thing this morning. Benny thought that would cheer up Buzz. And you know what? Benny was right. All that young man needed was a good night's sleep and some Aldens begging for his attention."

"He won't have to worry about getting our attention!" Jessie said on her way out back. "I'm going out for some basketball lessons, too."

Jessie wasn't the only Greenfield player who hoped to get some coaching from the talented twins. Word of their arrival had spread fast. Within half an hour, several neighborhood children appeared in the Aldens' backyard.

"You're so lucky," Patsy Cutter said when Jessie came out. "Imagine, Tipper Nettleton staying right in your own house!"

Patsy Cutter was a new friend Jessie and Violet had made. She was the best player on their team, the Fast Breakers, but she didn't have many friends.

"How come you didn't tell me about Tipper after practice the other day?" Patsy asked. "Are you and Violet keeping her to yourselves?"

"Grandfather didn't even tell us the twins were staying with us," Violet explained.

"Come on!" Patsy answered. "You just didn't want anybody to know."

When Tipper overheard this, she came over to the girls. She gave Patsy a big smile. "It's true. Mr. Alden wanted to surprise his grandchildren. Buzz and I were the surprise! I hope we live up to it."

Patsy just stared up at Tipper in amazement.

Finally Jessie spoke up. "Tipper, this is our friend — and teammate — Patsy Cutter. She's the best player on the Fast Breakers. Patsy, meet Tipper Nettleton."

Patsy's face grew red. "I . . . I can't . . . I can't believe I'm actually meeting you. I watch all your college games on television so I can play like you."

"Well, if you want, I can show you a few things now," Tipper said cheerfully. "You, too, Violet and Jessie."

"Go ahead, Tipper. It's okay to give Patsy a private lesson," Jessie joked. "We don't want to keep you all to ourselves."

"I hope Tipper teaches her about sharing the ball," Violet whispered. "Patsy never passes the ball to me. "It must be because I'm the youngest one on our team."

Jessie curled the end of her ponytail around her finger. She looked on as Tipper coached Patsy. "It's not just you, Violet. Patsy sometimes forgets she's on a team. Maybe Tipper will teach her more about passing the ball to other players instead of just making baskets herself."

A few minutes later, everyone looked up when three tall people walked down the driveway.

"It's Mr. Fowler, one of the referees who helps out with the teams," Jessie said. "Oh, and our coach is with him. I didn't know they were the basketball people coming over. I wonder who the other person is."

When Tipper saw the three visitors, she stared at the tall young woman in the group. Finally she stepped a little closer. "Hi, I'm . . . Oh, my goodness. I don't believe it! You're Courtney Post, right? Amazing! Are you one of the coaches for the neighborhood teams, too?"

The Aldens looked on, puzzled. How did Tipper Nettleton know their coach?

"Yes, I am," the young woman answered without a smile. "I guess we'll meet on the same side of the court for a change."

Buzz gave Tipper a gentle arm punch. "What do you know? You two old rivals meet again. But this time it's friendly, not like when Greenfield High played Warwick. Hi, Courtney, I'm Buzz — the other Nettleton twin."

Courtney ignored Tipper and turned to Buzz. "Hi, Buzz. I guess they didn't tell Tipper that she'll be helping me coach the Fast Breakers."

"Listen, I couldn't be happier, Courtney. Honest," Tipper said. "I always admired your playing so much, even though I feared it! Nobody made me lose more sleep over games than you. I hope we'll be friends."

Again Courtney ignored Tipper. What was going on? the Aldens wondered.

Courtney introduced the other people with her. "Frank, Tom, come meet the great basketball legend Buzz Nettleton. Buzz, this is Frank Fowler. He referees some of the games. As for Tom, he coaches the Rockets, one of the neighborhood teams. When he's not doing that, he works as a painter at the sports center. He's finishing up the paint job before it officially opens."

Buzz shook both men's hands. "Hey, I know you — Tom Hooper! Didn't you play for Warwick a couple of years before my class at Greenfield High? And Frank, I know I've heard your name."

Before Buzz could continue, Frank Fowler said quickly, "No need to go into details. Now that we've all met, let's sit down and get our plans organized. The kids in Greenfield are the big basketball stars now, not us."

"Yoo-hoo," Mrs. McGregor called out

from the kitchen window. "There's coffee and muffins in here. You can bring in your paperwork and work around the kitchen table. Everything's all set."

After the grown-ups went inside, Patsy Cutter began shooting baskets again. "Tipper just showed me a couple of new moves. Look how great I'm getting already!" she yelled as she made basket after basket.

Everyone else waited for Patsy to share the ball. But she never did. Finally the other players gave up.

"I'll get us some juice," Henry told everyone. "After that, let's have a half-court game."

Henry went inside to fetch juice and cups from the kitchen. He noticed everyone seemed awfully quiet around the table.

"Gee, you'd think they were talking about insurance or something boring — not basketball," Henry told the other children when he returned. "If I were famous players like them, I'd be going over all the great old games. They don't seem to care for one another much."

"Not like us, right, Henry?" Soo Lee grinned at her cousin.

"No, not like us," Henry agreed. "I hope Grandfather doesn't notice that they're not too friendly. He donated a lot of money to the sports center so people would have fun together."

Henry poured out juice for everyone. "My coach at school told me that when Buzz was a senior at Greenfield High, he broke Frank Fowler's record for the most points ever made. Maybe Mr. Fowler is still upset about that."

"That was such a long time ago," Jessie said. "He's a lot older than Buzz. Why would he still care?"

Patsy put her juice cup down on the grass. "Players always care about being the best. If I had the record, I would never, ever want anybody to break it. Oops, look what I just did." Patsy's paper cup had tipped over, spilling juice on her shorts.

"You can go to the upstairs bathroom and wash them off in cold water," Jessie said. "I have lots of shorts in the bottom drawer of

my dresser. Go ahead and borrow a pair. My room is next to the bathroom."

"Hurry back," Henry called out to Patsy. "We have enough kids here for a quick game."

After Patsy left, Henry organized the older children into two teams. "Benny and Soo Lee, you can keep score and be the referees. Whoever gets to ten points first wins."

Benny and Soo Lee took their jobs very seriously.

"Foul!" Benny shouted when a boy named James brushed by Jessie.

Soo Lee counted the score with some pebbles. The game was short and ended ten minutes later.

That's when Jessie noticed Patsy hadn't returned. "I wonder what happened to her. I'll go check."

Jessie scooted through the kitchen. She overheard Frank Fowler talking in a cross voice. "No, I disagree, Buzz. You haven't lived in Greenfield for a long time. It's not a good idea to team up kids from the south end with north end players. No way."

"Fine. Whatever you say, Frank," Buzz answered quietly. "Now, how about having Tom make up the practice schedules?"

Frank Fowler disagreed with this suggestion, too. "No, I have a computer at home, and Tom doesn't."

Jessie overheard Tom's nervous laugh. "Give me a paintbrush or a basketball any day. I'm not too good with computers and writing things down. It's okay by me if Frank handles the paperwork."

"Good. That's settled," Jessie heard Frank Fowler say.

Jessie headed upstairs. She checked the bathroom. Patsy's shorts were hanging on a towel bar in the shower. But Patsy didn't seem to be around. Maybe she had gone home without telling anyone. Jessie stopped by her room to get a stopwatch for Benny and Soo Lee.

When Jessie stepped inside, she jumped back. "Patsy! You scared me," Jessie said when she saw her friend standing next to Tipper's bed. "Oh, good, you found some shorts. I thought you went home."

Something heavy dropped to the floor.

"What was that?" asked Jessie.

Patsy looked worried. "I was, uh . . . looking at these pictures on this bookcase, that's all. A big book fell down. I'll pick it up."

"Fine," Jessie said. She went over to her desk for the stopwatch. She caught Patsy's reflection in the mirror. Whatever Patsy picked up didn't seem to be a book.

"Come on, let's go out," Jessie told Patsy. "Everybody's waiting for us."

CHAPTER 3

A Big Mix-up

Poor Mrs. McGregor. For the next few days she cooked up a storm for Buzz and Tipper. But the busy twins were hardly ever home!

"Goodness, those two are going to turn into skeletons," Mrs. McGregor told the children. "What they need is good home cooking, not all these banquets and such that they have to attend."

"Now, now, Mrs. McGregor," Mr. Alden said. "None of your delicious leftovers will go to waste in this house."

Benny patted his stomach. "See, I'm not turning into a skeleton."

Mr. Alden laughed. "Everybody in Greenfield wants to meet the twins before they start coaching the neighborhood teams. The newspaper is full of pictures of them visiting schools and youth groups. And they're going to be on television. I hope they don't wear themselves out."

Violet had been quiet all through dinner. Now she spoke up. "I hope Tipper has enough time for the Fast Breakers tonight. I need help on my passing. Courtney spends nearly all her time with Patsy. She's already a good player."

Jessie turned to her sister. "Patsy does take up a lot of the coach's time. Look, tonight is our first practice with Tipper coaching. I know she'll give everyone lots of attention. She wants to make the Fast Breakers into a super team."

"How are your Blazers doing, Henry?" Mr. Alden asked.

Henry seemed a little quiet. "Well, Grandfather, I can hardly wait for Buzz to start coaching my team. Then Mr. Fowler can go back to being the referee. He's been coaching, and for some reason he doesn't seem to like me."

"Frank is a hard one to figure out, isn't he?" Mr. Alden said. "When we were organizing the sports center, he was one of our biggest boosters. He had all kinds of plans."

"I know," Henry broke in. "Wasn't it his idea to have a fund-raising game with all the best players who graduated from all the high schools around Greenfield?"

"Indeed, it was his excellent idea," Mr. Alden said. "That's why I arranged for the twins to come back to Greenfield for a visit. Something changed with Frank after he heard about that."

Henry nodded. "Everybody thinks Mr. Fowler is upset that Buzz broke his high school record. Whenever anyone mentions Buzz, Mr. Fowler changes the subject. Anyway, things should get better starting tomorrow."

"Why is that, Henry?" Violet asked.

Henry studied a piece of paper. "Buzz left

me a copy of his coaching schedule. He's
due to practice with the Blazers tomorrow
afternoon. Mr. Fowler will be away at a
conference for most of the day. We won't
have to worry about Buzz getting in his
way."

The children helped clear the dinner
table.

"Well, I hope Courtney and Tipper get
along at our practice tonight," Jessie said,
handing Henry the dishes. "After all, they
were on opposite teams when they were in
high school."

"They're not too friendly, either," Henry
said as he loaded the dishwasher. "But at
least Tipper didn't break Courtney's high
school record."

An hour later, Mr. Alden drove Jessie and
Violet to the new sports center. The building wasn't quite finished yet, but the indoor
and outdoor basketball courts were ready
for practice. The Fast Breakers girls were
the first to use the indoor court.

"There's the twins' car," Violet said when

Mr. Alden pulled up. "That means they're back from the banquet. We're a few minutes early. Maybe Tipper can help me before the rest of the team gets here."

"See you later, Grandfather," Jessie said. "The twins are going to drive us home at nine o'clock."

The Greenfield Sports Center had a nice new smell of fresh paint and wood. Jessie and Violet stopped to look at the display case in the lobby.

" '*James Alden, Donor.*' That's Grandfather's name!" Violet said. "Now everyone who wants to play basketball can come here."

Jessie and Violet headed toward the gym. Their feet slapped against the new tile floors. Every sound echoed through the empty halls.

A minute later the girls heard angry words echoing through the halls as well.

"Somebody's having an argument," Jessie said.

The girls slowed down. Should they go in the gym? Or make a lot of noise so the people would hear them and stop arguing?

"It's easy for you to come in and take over for a couple weeks," a young woman said. "But I'm the one who's still going to be here after you leave Greenfield."

The halls were quiet. Jessie and Violet wondered what to do next.

"I'm sorry," the second person said. "I didn't want to force my ideas on the girls. I just thought —"

"Everybody knows what you think from all those interviews you do. But that doesn't mean I have to agree with everything you say. I still think we should pick out the best players and give them the most training. Then they can lead the team."

"That's Courtney's voice," Jessie whispered. "She and Tipper are having a disagreement."

Violet nodded. "Let's make a lot of noise so they'll hear us."

Jessie coughed. She and Violet took heavy steps. They didn't want to break in on the two young women during an argument.

Courtney and Tipper turned around when the Aldens walked in. Tipper looked flushed and upset. Courtney fiddled with some papers.

"Hi," Jessie said. "I guess we're early for practice. We saw your car outside, Tipper, so we just came in. Is Buzz here?"

Tipper cleared her throat. "He wanted to try the outdoor court now that the spotlights are hooked up. Then he has some errands to run. He'll be back to pick us up at nine. I wonder if I should go outside and practice, too. I don't seem to be much help around here."

Before the Aldens could say anything, some of the other Fast Breakers girls arrived. Courtney's and Tipper's cross words were soon forgotten. The girls squealed with excitement. Tipper Nettleton was really here!

One of the girls quickly removed a sneaker. She handed it to Tipper. "Hi, I'm Amy Billings," the girl said. "I know this might seem funny, but would you autograph my sneaker?"

Tipper laughed. "Sure thing, Amy." She picked up a pen from the coaches' table. "It's not the first time I've autographed a sneaker or somebody's hand or even a napkin in a restaurant. Here you go."

Pretty soon all the girls wanted their sneakers autographed. Suddenly everyone heard the scream of a whistle.

"Listen up, people!" Courtney yelled over the girls' voices. "Are we here to play basketball or get autographs? Anybody who isn't ready for practice shouldn't be here."

The girls' voices died down. They put their sneakers back on. Courtney blew the whistle again. The girls knew what this meant. No more talking. Make a circle. Listen to the coach. After all, they were the Fast Breakers. They wanted their team to be the best.

"Okay, we're going to do some drills tonight," Courtney told the players. "Tipper will take some girls. I'll take the others."

Several of the girls whispered when they heard this. All the girls wanted to be in Tipper's group.

But Courtney Post had other plans. "Okay," she began. "I want the following girls to line up here next to me: Patsy, Jessie, Mary Kate, and Ellen. Everyone else stand next to Tipper."

The girls stood in two rows side by side. Courtney and Tipper checked their clipboards to decide which drills to cover.

"What's the matter, Violet?" Jessie whispered when she saw how disappointed her sister looked. "Do you mind that we're not in the same group?"

Violet shook her head. "It's not that. Courtney just likes a few players best. She teaches them to keep the ball to themselves. I know you wouldn't do that. But the others she picked just hold on to the ball, especially Patsy. The rest of us won't get to play very much."

Jessie gave Violet's hand a squeeze. "Tipper won't let that happen. No way. Besides, now that she's coaching your group, you'll get so good, you'll be on the court all the time."

Courtney blew her whistle again. "Okay,

girls. Here's what's happening. Tipper will get some basketballs from the storage room. Everybody else, meet with your groups down at each end of the court. Ready?"

"May I have the key to the storage room?" Tipper asked Courtney.

Courtney stared at Tipper. "I gave you the key already. Don't you remember? Right after that newspaper interview here yesterday morning?"

Tipper's face turned red. "I'm sorry. I've been so busy, I guess I forgot. It's probably in my gym bag or my purse. I'll go check."

After Tipper left, Courtney spoke to the girls. "Well, it's too bad we have to waste so much time waiting around. We should be playing. But that's what happens when you're famous."

When Tipper returned, she was empty-handed. "I'm sorry, Courtney. I couldn't find the key. Are you sure you gave it to me? There were so many people around yesterday morning, I just don't remember."

Courtney shifted from one foot to the other. She checked her watch. "It's already seven-thirty. We haven't got time for this. There's a basketball in my gym bag. We really need a bunch of them, but one will have to do. I'll use it for my group. Did you bring one?"

"No, but Buzz did!" Tipper said, relieved. "He's practicing on the outdoor court — that is, if he's still there. I'll borrow his basketball. Wait up, girls!" she called out to her group.

A few minutes later, Tipper returned empty-handed again. "Buzz left. I don't think he'll be back until nine o'clock to pick us up." She look nervously at Courtney. "Do you think our group could share your basketball?"

Courtney rolled her eyes. She took a long time to answer. "I guess so. But you'll have to wait until we're done. Come on, girls."

With that, Courtney went off with her group. Soon the other end of the gym was filled with the sound of her girls dribbling, passing, and making shots from the foul line.

Tipper's group was quiet. When would

they get a turn? No one asked for Tipper's autograph now. The girls just wanted to play basketball. They weren't going to improve if they were watching from the sidelines.

"Sorry, guys. I really goofed," Tipper told the girls. "But that doesn't mean we just have to sit here. Let's do some stretches. Then I can show you some things my college coach taught me about the ready position and about guarding. You don't need a ball for those. Bet you've never played basketball without a ball before!"

Soon Tipper's girls were having fun even without the ball.

"First I'm going to show you the ready position. Okay, everybody, line up and do what I do."

Tipper stood with her feet apart, knees bent, arms out, and hands curved as if she were holding a ball. She made the girls practice their ready positions quicker and quicker. "Relax. Hold. Ready position! Now I want you to run, then get into position when I say stop."

In no time the girls were able to get themselves into the ready position without even thinking about it.

"Okay, the next drill is guarding," Tipper said. "This is important, girls. You need to be as close as possible to the other player, but you can't touch her. I don't want my Fast Breakers giving up foul shots to the other team. Okay, let's try 'ghosting.' Pair up with another player. Pretend one of you is running to the backboard with the ball. The other girl shadows the runner like a ghost. Remember, no touching!"

The girls enjoyed this drill. Tipper made them shadow each other closer and closer, faster and faster. When anyone touched, she blew the whistle, and the "ghost" was out. After a while, Tipper hardly blew her whistle at all.

"Gee, I guess you really can have fun playing basketball without a basketball," Violet said when the girls took a break.

Tipper bit her lip. She looked over at Courtney's girls. They showed no sign of giving up the ball. "Well, there's only half an hour left. It's even more fun to play with a ball! I'll ask Courtney for it."

At eight-thirty, Courtney's group finally quit.

"Everybody drink plenty of water," Courtney told her group when they stopped playing. She threw the ball across the gym to Tipper. "It's all yours."

Tipper jumped to her feet. "Okay, girls. Now you can try out everything we've been practicing, only this time with a ball. Ready?"

"Ready!" Tipper's girls screamed.

Soon they, too, were passing, dribbling, and making baskets.

A short half hour later, Courtney blew her whistle again. "Time to go home."

"Do we have to leave?" Violet asked when Courtney came over. "Our group didn't get much of a chance to practice with the ball."

Courtney pointed to the clock. "Sorry, the manager told me we had to get everybody out by nine o'clock sharp." She looked at Tipper. "Maybe next time somebody will bring the storage room key so the whole team can play basketball."

Tipper said nothing. Her girls were silent as they filed out of the gym.

"Patsy, could you get my ball and stick it back in my gym bag?" Courtney asked. "I'll be ready in a minute."

Patsy picked up the basketball. "Would you unzip Courtney's bag, and I'll stuff it in?" she asked Jessie.

When Jessie held the bag open, she noticed something. "Look at this." She held up a key chain attached to the zipper pull. "One of the keys says, '*Storage Room.*' Courtney had her own key the whole time."

Violet ran over to the coach. "Courtney! Courtney! We just found the storage room key. It was on your gym bag."

Courtney didn't say anything right away.

"Is it the key for the storage room of this gym?" Tipper asked Courtney.

"There are a lot of keys on the chain.

One is for the storage room of my apart-
ment building." With that, Courtney took
her bag from Patsy. "Next time, Tipper,
please bring your own key. The girls need
to practice."

CHAPTER 4

A Big Letdown

At nine o'clock the next morning, the Alden children and the Nettleton twins were sound asleep.

However, Watch was not sound asleep, not at all. He was wide-awake and scratching at Jessie's bedroom door. He had heard Grandfather Alden out in the hallway. He wanted to be up and about, too.

Mr. Alden heard the whimpering and scratching. He slowly opened Jessie's door. Watch scooted out and ran downstairs.

"I'm going out shopping today," Mrs.

McGregor told Mr. Alden when he followed Watch into the kitchen.

Mr. Alden took Watch's leash from the hook on the back door. "Have a good time, Mrs. McGregor. I'm glad all the young people are sleeping late for a change. This basketball fever is wearing them out. As for the twins — they've been on the go since they arrived. Henry said they don't have any practices or appointments until this afternoon."

Mrs. McGregor put on her hat. "Last night, Buzz and Tipper told me not to make breakfast," she told Mr. Alden. "They said they were going to sleep late, then surprise the children with breakfast at the diner."

Mr. Alden smiled. "That's just the kind of surprise my grandchildren like."

Nearly all of Greenfield seemed to be enjoying breakfast at the Starlight Diner when the Aldens and the Nettleton twins arrived.

"Hello, Aldens!" the waitress said. "I recognize you two," she told the twins. "I saw your picture in the paper last night. Welcome back to Greenfield."

"Thanks," Buzz said. "It's good to be back. Especially here. Our whole team used to come to the Starlight Diner for your famous burgers after basketball games. I hope you have room today. It's pretty crowded in here."

The waitress picked up an armful of menus. She waved everyone over to the back. "You just got lucky. A group of construction workers just left. The big booth in the corner is free."

Benny looked up at Buzz. "It's not really free," he whispered. "You still have to pay."

Buzz laughed. "Good one, Benny. Well, I'm glad we don't have practice until later, you guys. It felt good to get a couple extra winks of sleep for a change."

Soo Lee thought about this. "I don't wink when I sleep. I shut my eyes all night."

Tipper squeezed the little girl's hand. "I don't wink when I sleep, either, Soo Lee."

Everyone slid into the big booth and picked up a menu.

Benny didn't have to read it. "I already know what I want," he announced.

"Let me guess," Buzz said. "Liver and onions, right?"

"No way!" Benny cried. "Waffles with big holes to pour the syrup in. That's what I'm having."

That's what *everyone* in the booth was having. The Starlight Diner was famous for its waffles.

"Well, dig in!" Buzz said when the waitress set the plates down a few minutes later.

The booth was quiet while everyone ate their delicious waffles. But no one could finish them. In a short time, the children put down their forks.

"Our eyes are bigger than our stomachs," Tipper said.

"I was hungry. But even I can't finish these giant waffles," Buzz said. "We won't be able to play basketball if we're too full. Right, Henry?"

"Right!" Henry answered. "We'll be doing a lot of running and jumping. It's better not to eat too much. The other players can't wait to meet you. They keep saying how lucky I am to have my own private coach."

Buzz set down his glass of orange juice. "I wish that were true. Tipper and I haven't helped any of you Aldens much for the last few days. I'm not so sure I like being famous anymore. All these appointments and appearances sure get in the way of basketball."

"I know," Tipper agreed. "I'm getting forgetful, we're so busy running around. I forgot the key to the gym storage room yesterday. I'd rather play basketball than be on television."

"You would?" Benny said. "I thought you liked being on television."

"Not as much as I like coaching the team," Tipper told the Aldens.

"Same here," Buzz said. "That's really why I came back to Greenfield, not to have my picture taken all the time." Buzz checked his watch. "We'd better get on the move. How about dropping off Henry and me at the sports center? It's almost time for my first practice with the Blazers. I don't want to keep them waiting."

When Tipper drove up to the sports center, Henry noticed how empty the place looked. "No one seems to be around. I'll run in and check if anyone from the team is here yet."

By the time Buzz unloaded the car, Henry was back. "The doors are locked. Do you have a key?"

"Oh, no, not missing keys again!" Tipper said with a groan.

Buzz jingled something in his pocket. "Right here. Frank Fowler gave me a set yesterday. Let's check around. It's not noon yet. We're a little early. Why don't you kids get out and shoot a few baskets until the rest of the Blazers get here."

The Aldens followed Buzz and Tipper.

Buzz put his key in the lobby door. "Ta-da! See, I brought my keys, not like some people I'm related to."

Tipper didn't like hearing this. "Don't

tease me about that, Buzz. I feel awful that I let down the girls."

Violet slipped her hand into Tipper's. "You didn't let us down. We had fun. I learned a lot — how to guard people and how to always be in the ready position. We didn't need a basketball. We just needed you."

Inside the sports center, a few workmen were painting on finishing touches.

"Hey, there, guys," Tom Hooper said when he saw the twins walk in with the Aldens.

Buzz gave Tom a big grin. "Good to see you again, Tom. I'm here to coach the Blazers this afternoon so we can beat those fearsome Rockets of yours."

Tom pointed to the hall clock with his paintbrush. "You sure you have afternoon practice, Buzz? The Blazers were all here around ten o'clock this morning looking for you. I couldn't let them into the gym. So they all kind of straggled off."

"What do you mean, Tom?" Buzz reached into his back pocket. He pulled out a piece of paper and unfolded it. "Here's the schedule Frank gave me a couple of days ago," he told Tom. "Doesn't that say noon?"

"Sorry, I'm not too good at figuring out schedules and such," Tom said. "I just show up when somebody tells me to."

Tipper looked over Buzz's shoulder. "It does say noon," she agreed when she read the schedule. "I wonder why the team came early. Maybe you can call up some of the boys and ask them to come back, Buzz."

"Sorry, that won't work out," Tom said. "After you didn't show up, the other painters decided to do some touch-up work in the gym. The paint won't be dry for a few more hours. And tonight's no good, either. That's when I'm supposed to coach the Rockets in the gym. At least, I think that's what's on my schedule, if I can ever find it!"

Buzz looked upset. He checked the clock, then his schedule again. "I can't figure out what happened here. I planned all my appointments around this piece of paper."

"Try the outdoor court in back," Tom

said. "Some of the boys had a basketball with them. A few of them decided to wait for you out there. That was awhile ago, though. I don't know if they're still there."

When the Aldens and twins got outside, Henry mentioned something he had been thinking about. "Tom doesn't ever seem to know what's going on. Wouldn't he have a copy of the same schedule as yours?"

"I noticed the same thing," Buzz answered. "Courtney and Frank seem to organize everything. Maybe Tom's too busy getting the sports center ready to keep his mind on the plans."

As Henry neared the outdoor court, he recognized a few boys sitting on a bench nearby. One boy sat there bouncing a basketball slowly, over and over. The two other boys looked up when Buzz, Tipper, and the Aldens arrived. The boys just sat there and didn't say a word.

"Hi!" Buzz said. "I'm Buzz Nettleton, one of your coaches. I think there was some mix-up about our practice."

The boy with the basketball stopped

bouncing. "Yeah, there was a mix-up, all right. We have a schedule saying to meet for practice at ten o'clock. My dad dropped me off here early and everything. I even brought my new basketball for you to sign."

"Sure thing," Buzz said. He reached into his pocket for a pen.

The boy looked at Buzz. He began bouncing the ball again. "Never mind."

Buzz didn't know what to say. "Listen, guys, I have to apologize. I guess the schedules were changed and nobody told you. But that doesn't mean we can't practice out here right now. How about it?"

A car horn blew before the boys could answer.

"Our ride is here," one of the boys said. "Besides, we already practiced. We got a whole lot of practice just sitting around waiting for you to show up."

"I don't blame the guys," Buzz said after the car drove away. "Somebody gave us the wrong schedules. I don't know if it was theirs or mine, but I plan to find out."

CHAPTER 5

Jessie's Good Idea

That night Buzz and Tipper finally sat down to one of Mrs. McGregor's home-cooked meals. At last, no interviews. No banquets. No meetings or plans. Just a quiet evening with the Aldens.

A very quiet evening.

Mr. Alden did his best to cheer up the twins. "Mistakes happen," he said when he noticed that they hadn't said much during dinner. "You two have been on the go from the minute you arrived. It's understandable that schedules and keys and such got mixed up. There's still plenty of time to coach the Blazers and Fast Breakers before their games."

Buzz pushed his cake around his plate without taking a bite. "We don't have that many practices scheduled, Mr. Alden. And we got off to a poor start. Tipper and I shouldn't have been running around so much. Then all these mix-ups wouldn't have happened."

"Did you call Frank Fowler?" Mr. Alden asked. "After all, he's the one who made up the schedules, right?"

"I called him when I got back this afternoon," Buzz said. "He said he told me about the schedule change a couple of days ago. There was so much going on that day. Tipper and I had our pictures taken for the newspaper with some of our old high school teammates. There were so many people around, I guess I just didn't focus on what Frank said."

"Same with Courtney and the storage room key," Tipper added. "That day was a blur for me, too."

Buzz put down his napkin. "I've got to figure out some way to make things up to the Blazers — extra practices or something."

"Same here," Tipper agreed. "Coaching isn't just teaching basketball skills. It's pulling the team together. That's what I learned from my high school and college coaches. I want to be just like them."

All this time, the Alden children sat and listened. Just because of a few mix-ups, their new friends weren't having a very good time.

"I have an idea," Jessie said. "Do you both have a whole day free in the next couple of days?"

"Saturday we're free," Buzz said. "For some reason, we're not scheduled to be famous celebrities that day. No picture-taking. No television."

Jessie's face brightened. "Good. What about organizing the first-ever Nettleton Basketball Clinic for Saturday? We could hold it right here in Grandfather's backyard. You could schedule different drills for different times. I know we don't have a whole court, but you could teach lots of skills like you did with us when you first got here."

Buzz gave this some thought. "A clinic, hmmm?"

"Like a doctor clinic?" Soo Lee asked. "I don't want to get a shot."

This made everyone smile.

Tipper put her arm around the little girl. "You wouldn't get a shot, Soo Lee. But you would make a lot of basketball shots, just like you did the other day. A basketball clinic helps players practice skills one at a time. No doctors, no shots. Just fun."

Suddenly Buzz's face brightened. "You know, I brought some training tapes from my college. We could show those as part of the clinic."

"We can run an extension cord from the garage to the boxcar and hook up Grandfather's portable television and playback machine out there," Henry suggested.

The twins were all caught up in the Aldens' plans now.

"We'll mix up the teams," Buzz said.

"The Blazers and Fast Breakers can do the drills together with kids from other teams. A clinic just might help us make up the practice time our team missed. Good idea, Aldens!"

Tipper wondered about something. "Should we check with Courtney and Frank and Tom? I mean, a clinic isn't really part of the plans they have scheduled."

Buzz shook his head. "The clinic doesn't have to be part of the plans. Let's just call kids up and tell them about it. Anybody can come."

By this time Buzz and Tipper had spread out some paper and pencils to write down their plans.

"If we run the drills in sets, kids can start whenever they arrive," Tipper said. "We could probably fit in three sets of drills. That way it won't get too crowded in the backyard." Tipper put down her pencil. "Whoa, stop! We haven't even asked Mr. Alden if it's okay to fill his yard with all these basketball players."

Mr. Alden put down his coffee cup. "I

like seeing my yard filled with youngsters. Why, what's the good of having a big yard if people don't use it?"

Mr. Alden got his wish. By noon on Saturday, basketball players from all over Greenfield were in the backyard doing drills. In one part of the driveway, Buzz showed players how to dribble the ball while running. Tipper showed some older children how to make shots from the foul line. In the boxcar, Henry had set up Mr. Alden's portable television and a playback machine. About half a dozen players were inside the boxcar watching training tapes from Buzz's college. The clinic was a huge success.

"This is so much fun, I'm staying all day," Patsy Cutter told Jessie. "I want to be the champ of the Fast Breakers."

When Patsy went off to practice her foul shots, Jessie turned to Violet. "I was hoping Patsy would only stay for one set of drills. That's what I told everyone. More kids showed up at the clinic than we expected. Some players haven't had even one chance for Tipper to coach them."

Henry joined the girls outside. "Whew, I can't believe how many people are here. Buzz asked me to call up Courtney, Frank, and Tom. We definitely need more coaches!"

Right after Henry phoned the other coaches, a cameraman and reporter arrived from the local television station. The Nettleton Basketball Clinic was big news in Greenfield!

The reporter looked a little rushed and out of breath. "At last! I finally caught up with you two," she said to the twins. "My cameraman and I waited for you for about an hour at the sports center. When you didn't show up, we started calling around. We tracked you down here."

Tipper and Buzz looked confused.

"Why did you think we'd be at the sports center?" Buzz wanted to know.

"Didn't you get my message?" the woman asked. "I told someone at the center that we would meet you there at ten o'clock today and to call me if you couldn't make it."

Buzz shook his head. "We didn't hear a thing about this. We're in the middle of running a clinic. We really can't do an interview right now."

"Why not?" the reporter asked. "Your basketball clinic makes an even better story. After all, you did come to Greenfield to help out with the sports center. This clinic will give it even more attention."

"I guess we don't have a choice," Buzz told Tipper.

"Okay. First we want to film Tipper with her Most Valuable Player trophy," the reporter said. "Is it around?"

Tipper didn't move. "Can't you just show the two of us helping the kids? After all, isn't that the whole point of your coming here?"

"Sure," the reporter said. "But you're the first Greenfield player to get the MVP award. That is big news!"

"I'll go get it," Patsy Cutter offered when she overheard the reporter.

"You know where it is?" Tipper asked, surprised to hear this.

"Well, I saw it when Jessie and I were in her room," Patsy answered. "When I borrowed a pair of shorts from her."

"Good. Bring it down here," the reporter told Patsy.

When Patsy returned, the cameraman was taping Buzz showing several players how to dribble.

Patsy handed the trophy to Tipper. "Here it is."

Seeing this, the cameraman stopped filming Buzz and aimed his camera at Tipper instead.

"There," the cameraman told Tipper. "Just hold it like that while I get more tape rolling."

Buzz tried to get his players back to playing basketball. No luck. They all wanted to be on television. While the cameraman taped, several children stood near Tipper and waved or made funny faces at the camera. They were going to be on television, too!

"Buzz looks upset," Violet whispered to

Jessie when they came over to see what was
going on. "It's just like the day when we
kept asking about Tipper's award."

Buzz wasn't the only person upset about
Tipper's award. By this time, Courtney Post
and Frank Fowler had arrived to help with
the clinic. But there was no coaching, no
practicing, and no drills going when Courtney and Frank showed up. Instead everyone was watching the television crew
filming Tipper and her award. Finally the
cameraman waved Buzz into the picture,
too.

The reporter faced the camera. "And it
looks as if the Nettleton twins are headed
for victory again — not as Most Valuable
Players, but as Most Valuable Coaches in
Greenfield."

"Oh, no," Henry whispered to Jessie.
"Frank and Courtney won't like that."
Henry went over to them before any more
damage was done. "Thanks for showing up
on such short notice. We really need your
help. We didn't expect so many kids to
come."

Jessie tried to explain what happened. "The television people heard about the clinic when they went to the sports center. Then they came here. Buzz and Tipper didn't invite them. All they wanted to do was make up for the practices they missed. When so many kids showed up, they thought you might want to help out."

"Great timing," Courtney said. "We show up just in time to be in the audience for two coaches who don't even live in Greenfield anymore. I've got better ways to spend my Saturdays."

"Me, too," Frank said.

At last the television people left. The children flocked around Tipper to get a close look at her famous trophy.

"It's real silver," one girl from the Clipper team said.

"Of course it's real silver," Patsy Cutter told the girl.

"You should keep it in a safe place like a bank or something, with guards," another girl said, touching the tall, heavy trophy.

Buzz blew his whistle. "The interview is

over. Everybody who wants to do some drills, line up near the backboard."

"Right," Tipper said, sticking the trophy inside the boxcar. "Let's play basketball. That's what we're all here for."

"Anybody who wants to learn how to do championship layups should go with Coach Fowler," Buzz said. "He's the best layup player Greenfield ever had."

"Except for Courtney Post," Tipper said to the players who were trying to decide what to do next. "Her layups are amazing. Maybe Frank and Courtney can take over all the layup drills."

When they heard this, Frank Fowler and Courtney Post finally stopped looking so upset. Buzz and Tipper were famous for being famous. But Courtney and Frank were famous for their layups.

Buzz and Tipper moved out of the way of the two coaches. For the next hour they stayed in the boxcar, showing some of the kids training tapes. They wanted to give Frank and Courtney a chance to be the star coaches now.

* * *

By three o'clock, everyone was worn-out.

"What a day!" Henry said. "We had more people than at the sports center — almost, anyway."

"Thanks for coming," Tipper told Frank and Courtney. "We couldn't have done it without you. Especially after those television people showed up. That was the last thing we needed. From now until the sports center opens, all I want to do is coach basketball."

"Me, too," Buzz said.

"Mind if we take a look at the training tapes before we leave?" Courtney asked Buzz. "Frank and I want to see how your coach teaches defense positions."

"Sure, the tapes are on a shelf in the box-car," Buzz said. "Just pop them into the machine."

"See you Monday," Frank told everyone. "We'll turn off the television after we're done."

"So things worked out after all," Henry said after the Aldens went inside the house. "The clinic was a good idea, Jessie."

"Not a good idea — a great idea," Buzz said. "Except for all those TV people showing up, we taught everybody a whole lot of basketball."

The clinic had been a hit. The Aldens and the Nettleton twins decided to sit down and plan another one. They were so busy talking about what they would do next time, nobody paid any mind to Watch. He was barking and barking at the kitchen window.

"It's only Patsy out there, still practicing," Jessie said. "She's probably hoping you'll come out and coach her some more, Tipper."

Tipper yawned. "I'm all coached out. All I can think of is a hot shower and a nap. I'm afraid Patsy's on her own."

CHAPTER 6

Double Trouble

All the Aldens loved having the Nettleton twins as houseguests. But for Jessie, their visit was extra special. She was sharing her room with Tipper. Each night, after they turned out the lights, the two of them would talk in the dark until they drifted off to sleep. Jessie loved these cozy times.

"I feel so much better after running the clinic today," Tipper said. "I finally got to be the kind of coach my coaches have been to me. They taught me so much. Now it's my turn to teach kids what I know about basketball."

"I learned a lot from you and Courtney today," Jessie said. She stretched and yawned before curling up under the covers. "I'm tired, but it's a good kind of tired. That chair drill you did with us was fun. Sitting in a chair and trying to make baskets taught me how to stretch my arm way out and follow through."

"Follow through," Tipper said. "That's the key to everything — passing, shooting, dribbling."

Jessie's voice slowed down. "The key. I'm glad Mr. Fowler gave you that extra key for the gym today. Do you think Courtney ever gave you one in the first place?"

Tipper thought about this. "I honestly can't remember. I'm not going to bring it up with her again. All I want is for the two of us to work together. If only she would forget that we used to play on opposing teams."

"Courtney did seem a little jealous, seeing you with your trophy and all," Jessie said.

Tipper was practically asleep now. "That trophy. I can't wait until it's in a glass case at the sports center."

The room was almost silent now, except for Watch's gentle snoring.

Then Tipper sat up in bed. "Omigosh!" she said all of a sudden. "The trophy! I forgot all about it. Now, where did I put it after the TV people left?"

Jessie turned on the bedside lamp. The girls blinked at the sudden light. Tipper and Jessie stared at the bookcase.

"I forgot to put it back," Tipper said, fully awake now. She checked under both beds, then in the closet. "Let me think. After the interview all the kids were fussing over it. I thought it might bother Courtney and Buzz."

"I know!" Jessie cried. "You put it in the boxcar right before Courtney and Mr. Fowler started the layup drills. Remember?"

Tipper remembered. In no time, she put

on her slippers. "I'm going out to the box-car to get it now. Otherwise I'll be up all night thinking about it."

Jessie stepped into her slippers, too. She grabbed the flashlight she kept by her bed. Watch followed the girls down through the dark house.

The moon was shining. The backyard was all silvery. The girls tiptoed out to the boxcar.

Jessie slid open the door. She waved her flashlight this way and that. "I don't see it. Maybe somebody put it away for safe-keeping," Jessie told Tipper to make her friend feel better. "I bet that's what hap-pened."

"I hope you're right," Tipper said.

The girls returned to the house and went back to bed.

But Tipper didn't drift off to sleep easily. Her trophy seemed to have a curse on it. The curse wouldn't go away until she gave the trophy away. And she couldn't do that until she found it.

* * *

The next morning Tipper and Jessie stumbled into the kitchen for breakfast. They were pale, and they were both tired.

"My goodness, you girls look as if you haven't slept a wink," Mrs. McGregor said.

Mr. Alden looked up from his morning paper. "Maybe you should go back to bed and sleep in a little longer," he suggested. "Is anything the matter?"

"Tipper's trophy is missing," Jessie announced. "She put it in the boxcar yesterday. We went out there last night, but it wasn't there. It's not in my room, either. We're going to look around the house and outside now that it's daytime."

"Soo Lee and I will help," Benny said. "We're good at finding things. We have sharp eyes."

Tipper smiled for the first time that morning. "If anyone can find my trophy, I know you Aldens can."

But the Aldens had no luck, either. Benny and Soo Lee checked under every piece of furniture indoors and every tree and bush outdoors. The older children searched the garage and the back porch. The trophy was nowhere to be found.

"How did it wind up missing?" Henry wondered. "Everybody was around all afternoon yesterday. Unless . . . well, I mean, Frank and Courtney were the last ones in the boxcar. Remember? They were in there watching the training tapes."

Tipper twisted the corners of her napkin. She seemed about to say something, but the words wouldn't come out.

"Why don't we just call them up?" Jessie asked. "It can't hurt to ask."

Tipper was lost in thought. "It could hurt to ask, Jessie. If they didn't take it, they'll be upset that I suspect them. Buzz and I are just starting to get along with Courtney and Frank. Let's just wait until Buzz gets back. He had a meeting at the sports center this morning. I'll ask him if he's seen it."

Mr. Alden put down his newspaper. "I wish I'd known the trophy was missing. I drove Buzz to the center, but he didn't mention it. He should be back in a while. Tom Hooper is going to drop him off."

Tipper couldn't touch the food on her plate. "You know what? I'll just get restless waiting for him. I need to get out of the house. Jessie, why don't I drive you to that sporting goods store. I know you wanted to exchange those sneakers you bought for a bigger size."

"Good idea. Violet and I need some crew socks, too." Jessie ran upstairs to get her new sneakers. When she came back down, everyone was outside, standing by the twins' car.

"Here, put your shopping bag in the trunk," Tipper said, lifting the lid. "When all of you Aldens are in the car, there's not much room for anything else!"

Tipper was about to slam down the trunk lid when Buzz came into the backyard. "Hey, you found my hiding place!" he said. "It's not easy hiding things from you Aldens."

Tipper and the children stood in front of the empty trunk.

"What are you talking about, Buzz?" Tipper asked.

"Your MVP trophy," Buzz answered. "Isn't that what you're looking for? I stuck it in there yesterday. Patsy was showing it off to other kids in the boxcar. I got worried it would get scratched or something. Whoa, what's that look you're giving me, Tip?"

Tipper swallowed hard. "But why did you put it in the car? When the doors are unlocked anybody can pull the lever from under the front seat and open the trunk."

"I planned to go back and get it. But . . . well, I forgot. Sorry about that," Buzz said. He looked at the Aldens. "Hey, were you guys spying on me? Is that how you figured out it was in there?"

No one answered for a long time.

Tipper stepped away from the car. She pointed to the empty trunk. "There's no trophy in there, Buzz."

Buzz's face went white. His smile disappeared from his face. "What do you mean, it's not there? You're kidding, right?"

The Aldens moved away from the car, too.

"Take a look, Buzz," Tipper said. "The trunk is empty."

Buzz didn't speak. He went around, opened the doors, and checked inside the car. Then he looked under the car and all around the garage.

"Don't bother. The Aldens and I already checked every inch of the garage, the boxcar, the whole yard, and the entire house," Tipper told her brother. "We've looked everywhere."

Buzz stared at his sister. "Please don't look at me like that, Tip. I was trying to keep your trophy safe. Honest. That's why I put it in the trunk. It wasn't the best place, but I was going to bring it up to your room first thing. Then I got so busy, I forgot."

Tipper couldn't seem to look Buzz in the eye. She stood there and just stared down at her sneakers. "I guess it's my fault. I should have put it away myself. And now it's gone."

In a minute, Buzz was gone, too. He

walked down the driveway and disappeared down the street.

The children followed Tipper inside.

"What happened to your shopping trip?" Mr. Alden asked when everyone came into the kitchen. "Is something wrong?"

"Buzz took Tipper's trophy yesterday," Benny said. "But now he doesn't know where it is."

"I see," Mr. Alden said quietly.

Tipper tried to explain to Mr. Alden what had happened. "Buzz told me he saw Patsy showing off the trophy during the clinic yesterday. So he put it in the trunk and forgot to tell me. I mean, it's the most important thing I own. How could he forget? It's almost as if he wants it to disappear. And now it has."

Mr. Alden spoke gently. "Do you think he's done this on purpose?"

Tipper swallowed hard. "If it was anything else but the trophy, I would say no. We've always known everything about each other. That's the way twins are . . . until now. Ever since I got the award, Buzz has been different, not like his old self."

"He sure does act touchy about that trophy," Henry said.

"It's impossible to talk to him about it," Tipper agreed. "I don't want to accuse him, but this is the second time he's left the trophy in the car when it's been unlocked."

"Come sit down and have some breakfast," Mr. Alden said. "I'm sure we can help you figure this out."

Soo Lee patted Tipper's hand. "Benny and I are good finders. We found Violet's bracelet on the driveway."

"Once we found an old violin that was missing," Benny said. "And lots of other stuff people were looking for."

"What if we put up some Lost and Found posters?" Violet asked Tipper. "I could draw a picture of the trophy. I remember what it looked like."

This helped Tipper feel better, but only a little. "That's a good idea. Of course, if Buzz . . . Well, never mind. Besides, Buzz and I can't let ourselves think about the trophy too much — not with your championship games coming up. I'll just have to deal with it after the games are over. I'm going upstairs to rest."

Tipper left the kitchen. The Aldens could barely hear her footsteps. The children were quiet. Winning a big silver trophy sure didn't seem like much fun anymore.

CHAPTER 7

One-on-One

Over the next few days, Tipper and Buzz avoided the whole sore subject of the missing trophy. It was time to coach the Fast Breakers and the Blazers for the championships. The twins filled everyone's days with practices, clinics, and drills. If they were upset with each other, they tried not to show it. Basketball came first.

But the Aldens thought a lot about Tipper's missing trophy. They put Violet's Lost and Found posters all over Greenfield. Maybe somebody knew something about where it might be. They just couldn't accept that Buzz had anything to do with its disappearance.

"You know, Patsy was up in my room acting kind of funny the day she borrowed my shorts," Jessie said one afternoon when the twins were out. "She got all upset when I asked her about it. I feel funny bringing the subject up again, but maybe she had something to do with the trophy. After the other kids left, she was still outside playing basketball. Remember?"

Violet had some thoughts, too. "Well, lots of other kids besides Patsy were holding and touching it."

"If you ask me, Courtney and Frank Fowler could have taken it if they saw Buzz put it in the car," Henry suggested. "Look how bothered they are that the twins get so much attention. Too bad Tipper doesn't want to ask them about the trophy. I guess she doesn't want more problems with them."

"You're right, Henry," Jessie said. "Well, let's just hope someone who knows something about the trophy will see our posters and give us a call."

But no one called about the missing trophy. And the Aldens had very little time to think about it until the championship games were over.

More than anything, Buzz and Tipper wanted to help the Fast Breakers and the Blazers to win their own trophies. Every night before dinner they coached the Aldens for a few minutes.

"I hope no one gets too upset that you give us extra help," Henry told Buzz one evening when they were playing one-on-one in the backyard.

"Only a little extra help," Buzz said. "Besides, it gives Tipper and me some extra practice, too. No doubt about it, you Aldens give us a good workout. Don't forget, we have to be in good shape for our fund-raising game on Opening Day."

Henry zoomed past Buzz. "And it's . . . in!" he cried when his quick layup circled the rim then dropped through the net.

"Good one, Henry!" Buzz said. "If you make shots like that against the Hot Shots tomorrow, the Blazers will win the championship."

Henry and Buzz went in to get a drink of water. It was the girls' turn to practice.

Jessie and Violet went outside to wait for Tipper. They were surprised to see Patsy Cutter in the backyard. She was practicing shots from the foul line.

"Hi, Patsy," Violet said. She gave her friend a big smile. "You're just in time to practice with Jessie and me. Tipper will be out in a second."

Patsy didn't look too happy to see Violet or Jessie. "Some of the Fast Breakers think it's not fair that you get Tipper to yourselves all the time. I decided to come for extra help."

"It's okay with us," Jessie said. "Why don't you work out with Tipper by yourself? You're such a good player, Violet and I can learn a lot just by watching the two of you play."

This seemed to make Patsy feel better.

Soon Tipper joined her for some one-on-one basketball.

"I'm getting a real workout here," Tipper told Patsy as she tried to get the ball away. "You're pretty good at faking me out."

Patsy made another basket.

Violet and Jessie were cheering. "Good shot, Patsy!" Violet said, proud of her friend.

Patsy made one more basket. It went in. She'd beaten Tipper Nettleton!

"Great playing, Patsy," Tipper said. "Courtney's taught you a lot. The Blue Stars girls had better watch out. Thanks for playing with me. I need the practice before I meet Courtney across the court during the fund-raising game next week."

Patsy put her basketball in her sports bag. "Thanks, Tipper." She turned to Jessie. "I brought back your shorts. Do you have the ones I left here?"

"They're still in the upstairs bathroom," Jessie told her. "On the towel bar."

Patsy picked up her sports bag. "I'll leave these on your bed and go get mine."

Jessie got up, too. "I'll come with you."

"That's okay," Patsy said. "I know where to go."

"I have to get something, anyway," Jessie told Patsy.

Patsy reached into her bag. "Well, never mind. Here are the shorts I borrowed. I'll get mine some other time."

Jessie took the shorts. "No problem. I'll bring them to our next practice."

The next day, the Blazers and the Hot Shots met on the courts of the Greenfield High School gym, where the championship games were being held. Henry and his team were down on the court. Tipper and the other Aldens were up in the bleachers, waiting for the second half of the game to start.

The two teams were a good match. At halftime the scoreboard said Blazers, 22, Hot Shots, 22.

Buzz stood in front of the Blazers for a pep talk.

A player named Jake Reed raised his hand. "I didn't foul number fifteen. Hon-

estly, Buzz. But Mr. Fowler blew the whistle on me, anyway."

"And when somebody fouled me, Mr. Fowler didn't catch it," Henry said. "What do we do if it happens again?"

Buzz thought hard. He'd been playing basketball a lot longer than the Blazers. He knew better than to question the referee. "Just play the best basketball you can," he told his team. "Don't get too close to anybody. That way you can't foul them, and they can't foul you. If you play good ball the way I taught you, you'll make all your points without any fouls."

Halftime was over. The Blazers and Hot Shots circled for the toss-up. The buzzer went off. Henry tipped the ball to Jake, who passed it to another Blazer. Frank Fowler blew his whistle. He signaled for the Blazers to hand the ball over to the Hot Shots.

"I can't believe it!" Jessie said when Frank Fowler made this call. "The Blazers' ball was inside the lines when they passed it, right, Tipper?"

Tipper rested her chin on her fists. "Whew! I don't believe what I'm seeing, either. Frank Fowler keeps making a lot of calls against the Blazers."

"Is there anything Buzz can do?" Violet asked Tipper.

Tipper kept her eyes on the court. "Not much. If he complains, it might upset Mr. Fowler. All Buzz can do is help his players stay calm and play the best basketball they can."

That's exactly how Buzz coached the Blazers from the sidelines. Though Frank Fowler missed seeing several fouls against the Blazers, Buzz didn't question the referee. He just cheered on his team.

With a minute left in the game, the score was tied at 46–46.

The game went into overtime. The two teams went basket for basket during overtime.

Then Henry got the rebound. With just another few seconds left on the clock, Henry made a basket.

"It's in!" the Aldens screamed from their

seats. "The Blazers are ahead by two points!"

Tipper chewed on her thumbnail. "All the Blazers have to do is keep the Hot Shots from scoring. This is where all those guarding drills Buzz did with the Blazers will pay off."

The gym was wild with noise and cheering. The Blazers and Hot Shots had never played a better game. The Hot Shots player with the ball looked for chances to pass or throw. But everywhere he looked, a Blazer guarded a Hot Shots player. Finally the Hot Shots player tried to shoot.

"Foul!" Frank Fowler called out, pointing to a Blazer guard.

The Blazers fans groaned. No one had seen the guard touch the player.

"He didn't touch him, did he, Tipper?" Violet asked.

Tipper shook her head. "I know he didn't. Everybody else knows he didn't, too. But that's what Frank called. Now the Hot Shots guy gets two foul shots."

The gym was completely silent now. The

Hot Shots player stood at the foul line. He made his first throw. The ball bounced off the rim.

"Whew," Jessie said. "The Blazers are still ahead." She crossed her fingers.

The player took another foul shot. This one circled the rim for the longest time. Was it going to go in?

"He missed!" Tipper cried when the ball dropped off the rim onto the court.

When the final buzzer went off, the crowd seemed to explode.

"The Blazers won! The Blazers won!" the Aldens and other Blazers fans yelled and screamed.

The Aldens scrambled down the bleachers to the court. They hugged Henry. They hugged Buzz.

"You're the champions!" Tipper said, hugging Buzz over and over. "You guys did it."

Friends and family and sports photographers took pictures and talked to the team. Then the mayor came out and presented the boys' league trophy to Buzz. He passed it down the line to his players. Finally, when all the picture-taking was over, the Blazers left the gym.

Tipper and the Aldens waited outside the locker room. Henry and Buzz came out in their street clothes a few minutes later.

Buzz gave Henry a friendly punch in the shoulder. "Great game, Henry. You guys did everything I taught you."

"I did everything but guard people without having fouls called against me," Henry said. "I can't believe how many fouls Mr. Fowler called. I don't think the Blazers committed half of them, either."

Buzz slowed down. "Listen, that happens to the best of teams. You can't predict what a ref is going to do. Sometimes the calls go your way. Sometimes they go the other way. I have to say, though, that I've never seen so many fouls called that I disagreed with."

Everyone passed the lockers where the referees and coaches kept their things.

"Speaking of disagreeable, look at Mr. Fowler," Henry whispered.

Frank Fowler stood in front of a locker.

He was dumping his things into his bag. In went his whistle. In went his referee shoes. In went his striped hat. He finally picked up his bag and muttered to himself all the way out the door.

"Anybody looking at Frank Fowler would think he lost the game instead of refereed it. That's pretty strange," said Buzz.

"Well, Buzz," Henry said, "the Blazers won the game fair and square thanks to your coaching. There's nothing strange about that!"

CHAPTER 8

Sneaky Sneakers

When Jessie and Violet walked into the sports center the next day, Tom Hooper was up on his ladder painting the ceiling.

"Hi, Tom," Tipper called out. "Looks as if you're almost done. How are you?"

Tom didn't answer, so Tipper and the Aldens kept walking down the hall.

"Hey, wait!" Tom called after them. "I just remembered something. Frank gave me a note for you, Tipper."

Everyone turned around. Tom came

down from his ladder. He searched the pocket of his painter's pants. "Now, what did I do with it?"

"Do with what?" Jessie asked.

"Frank's piece of paper . . . mmm . . . let me see." Tom emptied his pockets but found nothing. Finally he picked up a piece of paper from the floor. "Whew. It fell out of my pocket. Frank says this is very important. Sorry, I almost forgot." He handed Tipper a paint-splattered, wrinkled note.

Tipper read it aloud.

Dear Tipper,
The Blue Stars' coach just came down with the flu. Since the Fast Breakers team has two coaches, you and Courtney, I have assigned Courtney to coach the Blue Stars until the championship game.

Frank Fowler

"Looks as if it's just us Fast Breakers chickens," Tipper told the girls.

Violet and Jessie looked at each other. They didn't mind this new change of plans

at all. They knew one thing: Practice with Tipper alone would be a lot more fun from now on.

All their other teammates, except one, cheered when Tipper announced that she was now the Fast Breakers' only coach. Only Patsy Cutter seemed to mind. She loved Tipper, but she also loved having two coaches to give her lots of attention.

All through practice Patsy followed Tipper around and begged for extra help. But that wasn't Tipper's way of doing things.

"Sorry, Patsy," Tipper repeated. "I know you want me to work with you on the power drill again, but that's a one-player drill. Today we're only doing team drills. Now that Courtney's with the Blue Stars, I have to work more with our whole team."

"But . . . but . . ." Patsy protested. "If the really good players don't get special drills, we might not be the best like you."

Tipper put her arm around Patsy's shoulders. "Being the best player means helping the team to be the best."

Patsy sighed. She couldn't help it. She

wanted Tipper Nettleton to herself. But Patsy didn't have any choice. She lined up behind the other Fast Breakers. It was time for a team drill.

The Fast Breakers practiced for an hour. Then the lights flickered on and off. The girls stopped playing.

"Time for the Blue Stars' practice," Courtney yelled across the gym. Her hand was still on the light switch. "It's two o'clock."

Patsy, Violet, Jessie, and some of the other girls went over to say hello to their old coach.

"I wish we still had two coaches," Patsy complained to Courtney. "I need special help. We only have one coach now. I can't work on my power drill or the wall drill."

"That's the way it goes," Courtney said, none too friendly to the Fast Breakers now. "Tell your teammates to move along. The Blue Stars have to practice now."

Right up to the playoffs, Courtney treated the Fast Breakers like strangers. If their practice ran over just a few seconds, she complained.

"Don't mind Courtney," Tipper told the Fast Breakers. "Some coaches are tough like that. They want everyone to be afraid of their team. That's the way Courtney's old Warwick High School team played. We were terrified of them. In the end, they won some games, and we won some others. It's two different ways of coaching."

"We like your way," Violet said.

Patsy Cutter wasn't so sure. "I like your way, too, Tipper. But don't you think it's a good idea to build up some players the other team is afraid of?" she asked. "You know — make some of us so awesome, the other team gets nervous?"

Tipper laughed. "Do you have anybody in mind?"

Patsy finally laughed, too. "Well, if you change your mind, I can be pretty scary."

Tipper Nettleton laughed. "I don't want scary players, just good ones like you who work as a team."

*   *   *

When the day of the championship game arrived, the Aldens were excited, but also a little nervous.

At breakfast that morning, Violet pushed her scrambled eggs around her plate, unable to eat them. "I can't believe we're going to play in front of all those people," she said. "I'm so nervous. I almost wish Patsy and Jessie and the other best players would play the whole game."

"Hush!" Tipper said. "Put that thought from your mind, Violet. I know what will make you feel better. Let's do a quick workout in back. When you see how well you practice, your confidence will bounce right back. Come on now."

Out in back, Violet tried out everything Tipper had taught her. Tipper helped her guard and pass and dribble and shoot until she was playing smoothly.

"You're right," Violet told Tipper when they finally stopped. "Now I know I can play against anyone, even the Blue Stars."

"Especially the Blue Stars," Tipper said before she and Violet went inside.

Jessie looked at the clock. "Only an hour and a half. What will we do until then?"

"Let's head over to the sports center to pick up our uniforms and basketball sneakers," Tipper suggested. "We have to take our things over to the Greenfield High gym before our game there."

"Good idea," Jessie said. "I'm too fidgety to stay home."

On the way over, Tipper helped the girls relax with some quiet music. "It's important to work yourselves hard, but it's also good to get your mind calm before a big game. That's what I always do."

But that wasn't what Courtney Post did with the Blue Stars. When Tipper and the Aldens walked into the sports center, Courtney was supervising some last-minute practice with two of her players. "Harder! Dribble it harder!" she yelled. "You don't want everybody to think you're the Blue Marshmallows, do you? Don't be afraid to look a little mean. It throws everybody off guard."

"They look scary," Violet whispered, starting to lose a little of her confidence.

"No, not scary, *miserable*," Jessie said.

Courtney noticed Tipper and the Aldens standing there.

"The office is unlocked," Courtney shouted at Tipper. "I sent my team's things over to the Greenfield High School gym with Frank. He's going to be the referee. We're leaving for the high school in a minute. Make sure you get your players there on time, too. You don't want to forfeit the game!"

"Ugh!" Tipper said with a groan after Courtney left. "Now, why did Courtney have to go and say that? I'm totally confident about everybody's playing. What I don't like much is getting everything ready — the equipment, the paperwork, the scoring sheets. I wish the sports center was ready so we could play the game here."

Violet patted Tipper's arm. "Don't worry. Jessie can help. She's always super-organized. She even lines up her slippers in one direction next to her bed every night."

Jessie laughed. "I thought everyone did that!"

The girls followed Tipper into the office. The room was still a little messy, with construction equipment cluttering up the small area.

"Can you get both duffel bags from the closet?" Tipper asked Jessie and Violet. "The uniforms and sneakers are in the bags. Oh, and grab a couple basketballs, just in case. You never know. I'll get the stopwatch and the papers we need for the game."

Jessie opened the closet door. "Did you mean this closet, Tipper?" she said. "There are only a couple of ladders and a bunch of paint cans in here."

Tipper came over. "Oh, no! The duffel bags were right here when we finished practice last night. I even put a name tag on each of them so no one would take them by mistake. I didn't want the team bags to get mixed up with anybody else's things."

"We'll go find Tom or Courtney," Jessie told Tipper.

"Tom? Tom?" Jessie called out. But the

only answer she heard was the sound of her own voice echoing back.

Violet ran to the lobby. She looked out the front doors. "Oh, no, Courtney just left."

Tipper and the Aldens were alone in the empty building.

"What should we do?" Jessie asked.

Tipper checked her watch. "Let's split up and check every unlocked room and closet in this building. Maybe the painters moved our bags somewhere else."

The girls split up. They raced through the dark halls. Most of the rooms and closets were locked.

When Violet and Jessie met Tipper in the lobby again, they were all empty-handed.

"All I can guess is that Tom or Frank took our duffel bags to the high school gym earlier," Tipper said, checking her watch again. "Let's keep our fingers crossed. We'd better get a move on. The game starts in about forty-five minutes."

CHAPTER 9

Go Team!

As she drove along, Tipper kept to the speed limit, but Jessie could see she was gripping the wheel. "I should have searched the office for a note or something," Tipper told the girls. "If Tom or Frank took our bags, they probably left a note."

"Maybe Mr. Fowler would, but Tom is so forgetful, I don't think he would remember to do that," Jessie pointed out.

When Tipper and the Aldens arrived at the Greenfield High School gym, they were disappointed. Frank had only delivered the Blue Stars' bags. The Fast Breakers' bags were nowhere to be seen, and the game was starting very soon.

"Finally!" Patsy Cutter said with relief when she saw Tipper and the Aldens. "The whole team was wondering where you guys were. They're in the locker room waiting for their uniforms and basketball sneakers. The Blue Stars are already out on the court warming up. What happened, anyway?"

"I'll tell you in a minute," Tipper said. "Ask the girls to meet me in the hallway outside the gym, okay? I need to speak to everyone without the Blue Stars around."

"There's not enough time," Patsy said. "We have to change."

Tipper took a deep breath. "I just need five minutes, Patsy. Please bring the team out to the hallway."

When Patsy passed back through the gym with the girls, Courtney and the Blue Stars were already warming up. They stared at the Fast Breakers. Why were they still in their street clothes? Weren't they going to warm up before the big game?

Tipper stood in front of her team in the hallway. "There's been a mix-up with the uniforms and sneakers," she began. "We're just waiting for Tom to show up. I'm counting on him to get here any minute."

"Are we going to forfeit the game?" Patsy asked. "We can't play without our uniforms or basketball sneakers. What's going on?"

Tipper shook her head. "I don't know. Sometimes I feel as if someone is making these mix-ups happen."

At that moment, Courtney came out. "It's less than half an hour to game time."

"We know, we know," Patsy said miserably to her old coach.

"Never mind us, Courtney," Tipper said. "We'll be there." Tipper Nettleton wasn't about to let this upset her girls. "Now listen. Remember the drills we did? I want you to take a couple of basketballs, then go to the outside court and warm up. Patsy and Jessie will coach you. The second the bags get here, zoom into the locker room, change, and get ready to play. We're going to win, right?"

There was a long pause.

"Right!" Jessie and Violet shouted.

"Right!" the others finally joined in as they followed Patsy and the Aldens outside.

Inside the gym, the bleachers were packed. Buzz and the Aldens noticed that only the Blue Stars were out on the court.

"Where are the Fast Breakers?" Henry asked Buzz.

"I'm going to find out," Buzz said. "Something's wrong. Tipper knows how important the warm-up is. Her players will be tense for the game if they don't practice first."

"I'll come with you," Henry said.

They found Tipper by a pay phone in the hallway. She was waiting nervously for a woman to finish a call. "Buzz, Henry — thank goodness you're both here. We may have to forfeit the game. The duffel bags with our uniforms and sneakers haven't arrived. Did either one of you see them the last time you were at the sports center?"

Henry's mouth dropped. "The team doesn't have its uniforms?"

"Oh, no! That's an automatic forfeit," Buzz said. "Do you want me to go back to the sports center to look for the bags?"

Tipper shook her head. "It's too late for that. I'm trying to reach Tom Hooper. He put some of the paint equipment in the closet at the sports center where I'd stored the duffel bags. I'm hoping he's on his way here with the bags."

At last the person using the pay phone hung up. Tipper dropped some coins in. She quickly punched in Tom Hooper's home number. She shifted from foot to foot.

Tipper put down the receiver. "Tom's not there. How can I break this to the team? They've practiced so hard. Hey, why are you smiling, Buzz?"

Buzz looked over Tipper's shoulder and kept on smiling. "Look who's running down the hall! And check out what he's got in his hands."

Tipper whirled around. Tom Hooper was

stumbling down the hall as best he could with a heavy duffel bag in each hand.

Tipper broke into a run. She grabbed the bags from Tom. "Thank goodness you're here! We were looking all over for you. I figured you had the bags. Where were you?"

"I went to Warwick High School," Tom confessed, looking a little confused. "When I asked Courtney where the game was, she said, 'The high school gym.' So I went to my old gym at Warwick High by mistake. That's where Courtney and I used to go to high school. Isn't that funny?"

No one was laughing.

Poor Tom. It took him a while to notice everyone's panic. "Uh-oh, does this mean you might forfeit the game?" he asked.

"Not if I can help it," Tipper answered. "Now you and Buzz go outside. Tell the team to hurry to the locker room and change. They've only got a few minutes to get out on the court."

The national anthem was already playing when the Fast Breakers finally appeared in the gym. Some of the girls hadn't quite pulled up their socks. Some sneakers were untied. But each of the girls stood tall and faced the Blue Stars across the way.

The big game was about to begin.

The Fast Breakers lived up to their name. When the starting buzzer went off, Patsy tipped the ball to Jessie. A tall Blue Stars player stayed on Jessie like a shadow. Jessie remembered all her training with Tipper.

"Look, she's passing the ball to Violet!" Soo Lee said from the bleachers.

"It's Aldens all the way!" Henry shouted. He was proud that his sisters got the ball so early in the game.

Violet was surrounded by Blue Stars players. The Aldens could see that she was nervous.

"Good, she's passing the ball back to Patsy," Buzz said.

"Do you think Patsy is going to shoot now?" Henry asked Buzz.

"I hope not," Buzz answered. "She's too

far away. She should pass it to Mary Kate. She's a lot closer to the basket."

Though Patsy was some distance from the backboard, she seemed about to shoot. Then she caught a glimpse of Tipper on the sidelines.

"Great! She's passing it to Mary Kate, and . . . it's in!" Buzz screamed. "Mary Kate scored the first two points!"

"Go, girls!" Henry shouted out.

"The Blue Stars are fantastic, but they're all over the place," Buzz pointed out at half-time. The Fast Breakers were ahead by six points. "Tipper's girls are like a drill team. They know all their teammates' steps plus their own. Way to go!"

"Can we go down and see the team?" Benny asked Buzz.

"You bet," Buzz said. "Here, I'll help you get through the crowds."

Down on the court, Buzz, Soo Lee, and Benny waited until Tipper finished her half-time pep talk. "You girls just keep playing the second half like the first. I know the Blue Stars are rough and tough, but they're getting tired. If I know Courtney, she'll keep playing the same few players."

"I'm not tired at all," one of the Fast Breakers said.

"Neither am I," several of the other girls mumbled.

"Hey, Aldens, how do you think we're doing?" Tipper asked.

"Incredible!" Henry answered.

"You're the best ones," Benny answered. "Even though you were late."

The whole team laughed when they heard this.

"Well, we're not going to be late for the second half," Jessie said. "Wish us luck."

"Good luck!" Buzz and the Aldens yelled.

The huddle broke up. Buzz and the Aldens returned to the bleachers.

The second half began. The game was never even close.

"The Blue Stars look as if they're running through Jell-O," Buzz said when the game was in the final minutes.

Soo Lee pulled Buzz's arm. "I don't see any Jell-O."

Mr. Alden and Henry laughed.

"They have rubber legs," Buzz explained to the little girl.

This made Soo Lee even more confused.

Benny knew what Buzz meant. "You know how when we get tired, we get floppy legs, Soo Lee? Like that."

"The Blue Stars are tired," Henry said. "Courtney doesn't rotate players the way Tipper does. So even their good players are making a lot of mistakes."

Henry was right. As the second half of the game went on, the Blue Stars made more mistakes than baskets. The Fast Breakers were on a streak. By the time the final buzzer went off, the score was 32–22. The Fast Breakers fans broke into a roar.

"Look, Soo Lee!" Benny said, pointing to the Fast Breakers down on the court. "The Fast Breakers have rubber legs, too. They're jumping up and down like rubber balls!"

"You were the best, Jessie," Benny said when everybody went down to congratulate the team.

"And you were the best," Soo Lee told Violet.

"The team was the best!" Buzz told his sister. "It was almost like those old Greenfield-Warwick games. They were great, but you girls were even better. Congratulations, everybody. Now go out on the court. The mayor is going to present your trophy."

The Fast Breakers stood straight and tall in a line in the middle of the basketball court. Flashbulbs went off all over the gym as proud parents and friends snapped picture after picture of the winning team.

Everyone quieted down when they heard the scratchy sound of a microphone.

"I am pleased to present the league trophy to the coach of the Fast Breakers, Tipper Nettleton," the mayor announced to the excited fans.

Tipper waved and smiled at the crowd. The mayor handed her the league trophy in one hand and the microphone in the other.

Tipper waited for the crowd to quiet down again. She looked at the crowd and held up the trophy. "I'm going to hand this over to my players to hold one by one. This league trophy doesn't belong to me, but to each of the Fast Breakers. They're a great team."

With that, Tipper gave the trophy to the first girl in the Fast Breakers lineup, who passed it to the next girl. The crowd applauded loudly as each girl held it up for the crowd.

The trophy reached Patsy Cutter, who was the last girl in line. But Patsy wouldn't take it. Finally the other girl gave up and handed the trophy to Tipper instead.

When the team went to the locker room to change, Patsy just got her things and left. Why wasn't she staying and celebrating with her teammates? In the excitement of their victory, the girls forgot about Patsy and just kept hugging and cheering. They were the champs!

CHAPTER 10

Lost and Found

That afternoon, there were two trophies on the Aldens' mantel. Mr. Alden took pictures of Henry, Jessie, and Violet standing with the twins in front of the fireplace. No one wanted to spoil the moment by mentioning that there were supposed to be three trophies in the picture.

"My lips ache," Tipper said after everyone had finished posing. "I've never smiled so much in one day as I did today."

"Same here," said Buzz. "But save a few smiles for Great-Aunt Nora. We promised to be at her house in fifteen minutes. Let's go."

The Aldens followed the twins out to their car. The twins were going to visit some relatives for a couple of nights.

"So long, everyone," Tipper said. "See you on Opening Day, trophy or no trophy."

"Wait a moment," Mr. Alden called out when he noticed a letter for Tipper in the mailbox. "Here's a letter for you."

"What an odd envelope." Tipper tore it open. "It's written in big block letters without a return address." She unfolded the sheet of notebook paper inside. "Goodness!" she cried. "Listen:

" '*Your trophy is safe. You will find it at the sports center on Opening Day.*' "

Tipper's face grew pale. "Do you know anything about this?" she asked Buzz.

"Why are you asking me?" Buzz wanted to know. He started the car up. "Let's not talk about this now. I don't want to ruin our visit with Great-Aunt Nora."

"Leave the note with us," Jessie whispered. "Maybe we can figure it out."

Tipper gave Jessie the note. After the twins drove off, Soo Lee and Benny held the piece of paper up to the sunlight.

"No fingerprints," Benny said. "But know what? If we find out who writes like this, maybe we can find Tipper's missing trophy."

Soo Lee didn't mean to giggle, but she couldn't help it. "I write in big letters! But I don't know all my letters yet."

The Aldens laughed over this, though Tipper's missing trophy was no laughing matter.

The Aldens spent the next day decorating the sports center with balloons and streamers. They made signs showing where the celebrations were going to be. They set up the tables and chairs for refreshments. And the whole time they worked, they kept their eyes open for Tipper's trophy.

"I just went into Mr. Fowler's office to ask about the folding chairs," Henry told Jessie and Violet when he saw them putting up posters on a bulletin board.

"While Henry was talking, Soo Lee and I peeked on his desk," Benny whispered. "But we didn't see any pieces of paper like Tipper's letter."

"He writes with eensy-weensy letters," Soo Lee added. "Not big, giant letters. We peeked in the closet, too, but there were only old paint cans in there."

Jessie smiled. "Good work, you two. I just hope whoever wrote that note is right — that the trophy will be here tomorrow. But I sure would like to find it ahead of time."

"Hey, Aldens," the children heard Tom Hooper call out when he saw them. He set a messy stack of papers on the floor. "Here, use some double-sided tape, Jessie. That works better than plain tape for putting up signs."

While Tom helped Jessie, Soo Lee and Benny pretended to pick up something from the floor.

"Thanks," Tom said when he saw Benny and Soo Lee gathering up his papers. "So long, now. Just throw the tape in my toolbox when you're done, Jessie. It's in the office closet with my painting gear."

"Tom didn't have any paper like that note," Benny whispered after Tom left. "And he has little bitsy handwriting, too."

When the Aldens went to the office, Courtney was talking on the phone.

Jessie held up the roll of tape. "Don't hang up. We're just putting this back in Tom's toolbox."

By this time Courtney had hung up the phone. "Fine, just shut the office door when you leave. And don't touch anything on this desk."

So they didn't. Instead, Benny and Soo Lee tried to see if any paper on Courtney's desk matched the paper the mystery writer had used.

"Nope," Benny said, looking over but not touching anything.

Outside, a cleaning person was pushing a cart down the hall.

"Look what fell off." Henry picked up a sheet of paper with red marker letters on

top. "It's an old practice schedule for the Blazers. It says, '*Give to Buzz.*' "

Jessie looked over Henry's shoulder. "It's the schedule Buzz was supposed to get for the first practice. I guess Mr. Fowler forgot to give it to Buzz. Maybe the mix-up wasn't on —"

"On purpose!" the Aldens heard Mr. Fowler say. "So that's what everybody thinks? That I made things hard for Buzz Nettleton?"

The Aldens didn't speak. They *did* believe Mr. Fowler made things hard for Buzz on purpose.

"Everybody's wrong thinking I'm out to get Buzz. I had the record for ten years before he broke it. I knew somebody was going to break my record someday."

By this time Courtney had come out to see what the commotion was all about. She overheard Frank getting upset. "You know what's hard?" she asked, looking at the Aldens. "That everything Frank and I did was pushed aside just because the Nettleton twins came back. Frank and I worked with the neighborhood teams for months. Then the twins showed up. Pretty soon all we were good for was making up schedules and such."

"The twins are leaving in a couple of days," Mr. Fowler said. "But we'll still be here. Only there aren't any newspapers and television people looking to talk to us."

The Aldens felt awful. Frank Fowler and Courtney Post had worked hard with the teams.

"What about our game?" Henry asked. "It seemed like you wanted the Blazers to lose just because Buzz was coaching us."

Mr. Fowler was quiet now. "I'll admit I made a lot of bad calls during the game. I should have let Tom referee the game, but he can get so distracted. He even forgot to give Buzz this schedule change. Not to mention the mix-up with the television people I found out about. Tom took the message from them but forgot to tell the twins about it. So the crew showed up at the sports center and no one was there."

Henry still wanted to know what happened at the Blazers game. "Were you upset with our team?"

"In a way I was," Mr. Fowler said. "I let my own jealousy get me in a bad mood. I guess I took it out on your team. For sure, I wasn't thinking straight during that game. I'm sorry about that. But, hey, guess what?"

"The Blazers won the trophy anyway!" Henry said proudly. "Speaking of trophies . . ."

Courtney shrugged her shoulders. "Hey, don't look at me. I'm sorry about what happened at our first practice. I found Tipper's keys and kept them. I . . . well . . . I was afraid the team would like her better than they liked me. I tried to make her look disorganized in front of the girls. But I didn't have anything to do with that missing trophy. I still have one more year of college. I'd rather win my own trophy than take it from Tipper. She's taught me a lot about how to be a good team player. Maybe next year I'll be the Most Valuable Player!"

The next day, the Aldens dressed up in their basketball uniforms. Mr. Alden whistled while he put on his most colorful bow tie.

"Why such long faces?" he asked when he noticed no one else seemed very excited about Opening Day. "I know you're wondering about that trophy. But we must trust the writer of that letter and hope for the best. Now let's head out. We don't want to be late!"

The parking lot was packed when Mr. Alden drove up to the sports center. People were streaming into the brand-new building. There were balloons inside the lobby. The Aldens could hear the Greenfield High School band playing inside the gym.

"Your decorations look very fine," Mr. Alden told his grandchildren. "I see Nora Nettleton going in. The twins must be here already. I'll meet you all in the front row of the gym. I'll be with the twins and some of their Greenfield relatives and friends."

Soo Lee tugged Jessie's sleeve. "I forgot to brush my hair."

"Me, too." Benny tried to flatten a curl of hair that just wouldn't stay down.

Jessie took the younger children by the hand. "I'll bring you both to the locker room so you can get nice and spiffy. But first, Benny, take this envelope to the referee. Patsy wrote up the team's names, numbers, and records for the game."

Benny took the envelope from Jessie. He tried to read the words. "Fast Breakers Statis . . . What's this hard word?" Before Jessie could answer, Benny noticed something else. "Hey! Look at the letters on this envelope! Where's that note about the missing trophy? I think the letters are the same!"

Jessie reached into her gym bag. She pulled out the crumpled note and smoothed it out.

"Look. It's the same printing as on this envelope!" Benny cried.

"I bet if we find Patsy, we'll find Tipper's trophy," Jessie said.

"I saw Patsy go up that staircase about ten minutes ago," Henry said when he overheard the children talking. "There's another locker room on the second floor."

Soo Lee and Benny raced up the stairs with Jessie and Henry following right behind.

The halls leading to the locker room were dark. But Jessie knew the way. She pushed open the door and searched for the light switch. But she couldn't find it. The children followed her into the darkened room.

The Aldens were not alone. They stood still. There was just enough light to see someone standing in front of a large wall mirror — someone holding a tall, silver trophy!

"Patsy!" Jessie cried out.

Patsy jumped when she saw the Aldens' reflection. She quickly put the trophy under one of the benches.

"Where did you find that?" Violet asked.

Patsy didn't answer.

"We've been searching for that ever since it disappeared," Henry said.

"I'm the one who took it from the trunk of the twins' car after I saw Buzz put it there," Patsy told Henry.

"Why?" Jessie asked, her voice shaking.

Patsy took a deep breath. "I just wanted to have it overnight — without anyone around. I tried to get it back to your room, Jessie. But you kept following me."

Jessie picked up the trophy from under the bench.

"I saw Tipper on television when she won it last month," Patsy continued. "I couldn't believe she was actually in Greenfield coaching our team. I thought if I borrowed her trophy, some of her talent might rub off on me. I want to be a great player like her — and Courtney, too."

"Why didn't you tell her?" Soo Lee asked.

Patsy went on, "I tried to get it back to her, but it was never the right time. Then, when our team won the league trophy, I felt worse. Tipper helped us win it, and I had taken hers. So I sent her the note and planned to bring it back today without getting caught."

"Well, here it is!" Jessie said. "We'd better bring it to the gym right away. Tipper would be pretty embarrassed if the mayor called her to the gym floor and she was empty-handed. You can tell her the whole story later."

Soo Lee forgot all about brushing her hair. Benny forgot about the curl that wouldn't behave. None of it mattered.

When the Aldens walked into the gym with Patsy, they held up the trophy so Tipper could see it. The spotlights made the silver reflect all over the gym. Tipper gave Patsy and the Aldens a thumbs-up sign.

When Patsy and the Aldens entered the gym, the band was playing the Greenfield High School fight song. Cheerleaders were tumbling and doing somersaults in front of the crowd.

The mayor tapped the microphone, which made a horrible scratchy sound. "Ladies and gentlemen," the mayor said, "may I present Tipper Nettleton, the Most Valuable Player in the country. She will now donate her trophy to our new sports center."

Jessie handed Benny the trophy. "Go ahead. Take it down to her."

Benny ran down to the gym floor. He held up the trophy. The mayor gave him the microphone. In a voice just like the mayor's, Benny said, "May I present Tipper Nettleton with the most valuable trophy that was ever missing."

All of the Aldens laughed, and the whole audience joined in. Benny laughed harder than anyone.

GERTRUDE CHANDLER WARNER discovered when she was teaching that many readers who like an exciting story could find no books that were both easy and fun to read. She decided to try to meet this need, and her first book, *The Boxcar Children*, quickly proved she had succeeded.

Miss Warner drew on her own experiences to write the mystery. As a child she spent hours watching trains go by on the tracks opposite her family home. She often dreamed about what it would be like to set up housekeeping in a caboose or freight car — the situation the Alden children find themselves in.

When Miss Warner received requests for more adventures involving Henry, Jessie, Violet, and Benny Alden, she began additional stories. In each, she chose a special setting and introduced unusual or eccentric characters who liked the unpredictable.

While the mystery element is central to each of Miss Warner's books, she never thought of them as strictly juvenile mysteries. She liked to stress the Aldens' independence and resourcefulness and their solid New England devotion to using up and making do. The Aldens go about most of their adventures with as little adult supervision as possible — something else that delights young readers.

Miss Warner lived in Putnam, Connecticut, until her death in 1979. During her lifetime, she received hundreds of letters from girls and boys telling her how much they liked her books.